Jack
and the
Beanstalk

Retold by Katie Daynes

Illustrated by
Paddy Mounter

Reading consultant: Alison Kelly
Roehampton University

Contents

Chapter 1

Cow for sale

Jack was very, very hungry.
He searched the house for
something to eat. But he didn't
find anything, not even a bean.

3

Jack and his mother were
very poor. They lived alone in
a little cottage. The only
thing they owned was a cow
named Milky White.

Moooo

And she was
so old, she'd
run out of milk.

4

"Can't you make yourself useful?" asked Jack's mother, brushing past with a broom.

"But there's nothing to do," complained Jack.

Why don't you milk Milky White?

She has no milk left.

Jack's mother stopped sweeping and sat down. "We have nothing," she sighed. "Nothing to eat, nothing to drink, nothing to sell... nothing."

"Except Milky White," Jack pointed out. There was a long pause, followed by a low tummy grumble.

"Alright," said Jack's mother. "Tomorrow, you must take Milky White to market. Get the best price you can."

Easy!

Finally, Jack had a job to
do. At the first sign of dawn,
he ran outside.

"Morning, Milky White," he
said. "We're going to market."

"Moo," said Milky White.
She didn't understand a word.

They hadn't gone far
when they met an old man.

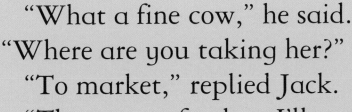

"What a fine cow," he said.
"Where are you taking her?"
"To market," replied Jack.
"Then go no further. I'll
buy her." The old
man reached deep
into his pocket
and took out...

five dried
beans.

"Beans?" said Jack.

"*Magic* beans," answered the man. "Plant them today and you'll see a beanstalk reaching to the clouds by morning."

"Wow! That's amazing," said Jack. "And you'll give them to me for old Milky White?"

The old man nodded.
"It's a deal!" Jack cried. He grabbed the beans, handed over Milky White, thanked the man and ran off.

Chapter 2

The beanstalk

On the way home, Jack looked closely at the beans. "They don't look magic," he thought, frowning. "Oh dear, what's mother going to say?"

He soon found out.

"You're back early," called his mother. "How much did you get for Milky White?"

Jack didn't dare answer. Instead, he opened his fist and showed her the beans.

His mother was furious. She threw the beans to the ground and sent Jack to his room. "Thanks to you, there's no lunch or supper," she yelled.

Jack hid under his blanket, feeling foolish. Finally, night came and he fell asleep.

When he woke up, his
room was still dark. But he
could hear birds chattering.
"Strange..." he thought,
and went to the window.
A thick curtain of leaves
blocked out the sun. He
looked closer and saw a
massive plant, reaching
up to the sky.

A beanstalk!

He raced downstairs and
bumped into his mother.
"Hello," he said, timidly.
"What have you done to
my garden?" she screeched.
Jack rushed past her.
He wanted to climb his
beanstalk.

The twisted shoots made a good ladder. Soon Jack's house was nothing but a dot and he was feeling rather dizzy.

"I'll just climb as far as the clouds," he decided.

Chapter 3

Above the clouds

At last, Jack's hair brushed a soft, fluffy cloud. He climbed a little higher and almost fell off the beanstalk in surprise.

There, floating in the
distance, was an enormous
castle. A delicious smell of
sizzling sausages drifted
through the air.

"Breakfast!" thought Jack, hungrily. He was clambering onto the cloud when he heard a little voice.

"Be careful," it said, sweetly.

Jack saw a tiny figure with wings and a wand. "I don't believe in fairies," he thought. He blinked hard, but the fairy was still there.

"A terrifying giant lives in that castle," warned the fairy. "He killed your father."

"A *giant* killed my father?" gasped Jack.

Didn't your mother tell you?

"He was a brave man," she sighed. "One day, the greedy giant attacked a flock of sheep. Your father rushed to protect them... and the giant ate him."

21

Just then, a whiff of bacon
made Jack's nose twitch.
"I'm going to pay this giant
a visit," he told the fairy.

Oh yes
I am.

Oh no
you're not.

Jack marched up to
the castle. He wanted to feel
brave like his dad, but he just
felt hungry. Suddenly, the
castle door began to open.

Jack hid behind a flowerpot. A giant woman appeared, carrying a giant watering can.

Pah!

Then a giant drop of water splashed on Jack's head... and drenched him.

"Help!" he gargled.

"Oh, sorry deary," said the giant woman. "I didn't see you. Come inside to dry off."

She plucked Jack from the ground, sat him on the palm of her hand and sailed him through the vast castle corridors.

24

Chapter 4

Fee fi fo fum...

In no time, Jack was sitting
on the kitchen table.

"One sausage or two?"
asked the giant woman.

Jack gulped. Each sausage was as long as him. "Umm... half please," he answered.

He was smearing butter on his third toasted crumb when he heard a thunderous **ROAR!**

"Oh no," cried the giant woman. "That's my husband. If he sees you, deary, *you'll* be breakfast..."

She hid Jack in an empty teapot. Heavy footsteps shook the room.

"Fee, fi, fo, fum," bellowed a rumbling voice. "I smell the blood of a little man..."

Jack slowly lifted the teapot lid. A **GIANT** giant was stomping around the kitchen, sniffing the air greedily.

"That monster killed my father," thought Jack, terrified.

"Be he alive or be he dead, I'll grind his bones to make my bread!" the giant boomed.

"I'm sure you will, dear," replied the giant's wife. "But eat your breakfast first."

The giant soon forgot Jack's smell. He guzzled down every mouthful, then licked his plate clean. "Bring me my hen," he ordered his wife.

She placed a little hen on his hand. Jack watched as it clucked, flapped its feathers and laid a shiny golden egg.

"Another!" growled the giant. "And another!" Eggs piled up on his hand, glinting in the morning light.

The giant looked very pleased with himself. Then he yawned. He rested his chin on the table and nodded off.

z z z z z z z z z

"Time to escape," thought Jack. He clambered out of the teapot and dropped down, just by the giant's hand. The little hen stood trembling by her gold eggs.

You're coming too!

Jack grabbed the hen, slid down the tablecloth and raced through a crack under the door.

A giant dog barked loudly but Jack kept running. He heard the giant's angry roar and ran even faster.

At last, the beanstalk was in sight. Jack flung himself at it and scrambled down to safety.

Chapter 5

Another adventure

When Jack's mother saw the hen, she licked her lips. "Mmm, chicken for dinner," she said.

"No way!" cried Jack. "This hen lays gold eggs. She'll make us rich."

"Of all the silly stories…" Jack's mother began.

Just then, the hen clucked, flapped her feathers and laid a golden egg.

We're rich!

It's true!

An egg a week bought Jack and his mother all they needed. Life was very comfortable, but also a little dull.

One morning, Jack was lying in the shade of the beanstalk, when the smell of sizzling sausages wafted by.

36

He looked at the
beanstalk towering above,
then he looked at the
giant's magic hen.

"Maybe the giant has
other treasures," thought
Jack. "I think it's time for
another adventure..."

The beanstalk
seemed much higher
than before. When
Jack touched the
clouds, he was
already puffing
and panting.

He followed the smell of sausages to the castle kitchen and crept under the door. The giant's wife was whistling by the stove.

"Please Mrs. Giant," called Jack, politely, "do you have half a sausage to spare?"

"Go away," she said. "The last boy stole my husband's hen. Gerald is still in a terrible temper. If he finds you here, he'll gobble you up."

"Oh," said Jack, turning to leave. "Sorry to bother you..."

"Wait," she said, kindly. "I'm sure I can find you something."

Jack was munching on a fried mushroom, when a giant voice echoed around the room.

FEE FI
FO
FUM

Jack dived into the sugar. "I smell the blood of a little man," boomed the giant.

41

"You're imagining things, Gerald," replied his wife. "I'll fetch your harp. That will calm you."

As the angry giant sniffed around the room, his wife placed a tiny, golden harp on the table. It played soft, soothing tunes, all on its own.

The giant sat down,
closed his eyes and
began to snore.

zzzzzZZZZ

"Quick, go,"
whispered
his wife
to the
sugar
bowl.

Jack leaped out.
Seeing the beautiful
harp, he tucked
it under his arm
and fled.

The music
stopped and
the giant woke
up. "My harp!"
he cried. Seconds later,
he was pounding after
Jack. "I'll grind your
bones, you little thief!"

Quick! He's
behind you!

As Jack hurried
down the beanstalk,
it began to sway.
The giant was
climbing down too.

44

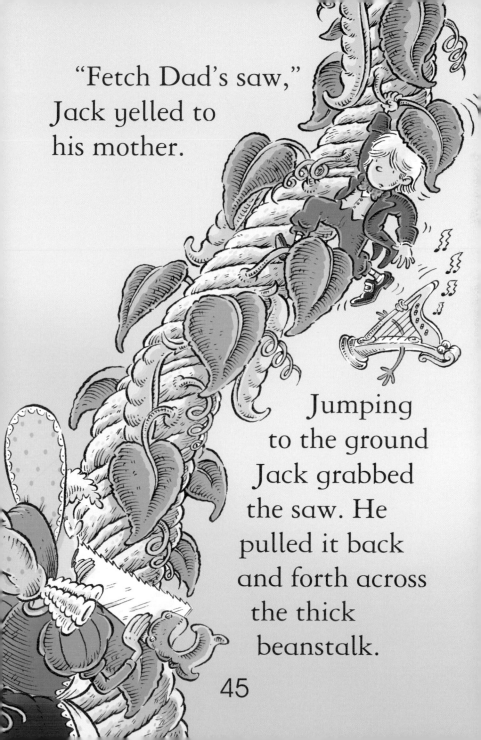

"Fetch Dad's saw," Jack yelled to his mother.

Jumping to the ground Jack grabbed the saw. He pulled it back and forth across the thick beanstalk.

45

Suddenly, there was a massive **CREAK**. The whole beanstalk toppled to the ground, flinging the giant over the distant hills.

No one ever saw him again.

With a hen that laid gold
eggs and a beautiful singing
harp, Jack and his mother
lived very happily.

But sometimes Jack found
himself gazing at the
beanstalk stump, wishing that
it would grow once more.

No one knows where the story of
Jack and the Beanstalk comes from, but people
have been telling it for hundreds of years.
Today it's also a popular pantomime tale.

Series editor: Lesley Sims
Designed by Natacha Goransky
and Louise Flutter
Cover design: Russell Punter

First published in 2006 by Usborne Publishing Ltd., Usborne House,
83-85 Saffron Hill, London EC1N 8RT, England. www.usborne.com
Copyright © 2006 Usborne Publishing Ltd.

48